SOCK MONKEY RIDES AGAIN

Cece Bell

CANDLEWICK PRESS

For Charlie and Oscar, and their granddaddies

First edition in this format 2015

Library of Congress Cataloging-in-Publication Data is available.

Library of Congress Catalog Card Number 2006040086

ISBN 978-0-7636-3089-8 (original hardcover)
ISBN 978-0-7636-7760-2 (reformatted hardcover)

15 16 17 18 19 20 CCP 10 9 8 7 6 5 4 3 2 1

Printed in Shenzhen, Guangdong, China

This book was typeset in Cafeteria.
The illustrations were created digitally.

Candlewick Press
99 Dover Street
Somerville, Massachusetts 02144

visit us at www.candlewick.com

One day, Sock Monkey, the famous toy actor, received a very important telephone call.

Hello?

You're WANTED FOR THE PART OF "RED REARDON" IN OUR SINGING COWBOY MOVIE, "HUBBUB AT THE HAPPY CANYON HOEDOWN"!

Sock Monkey didn't want to kiss a girl. But he did want to be a star. Sure, he had acted in other movies – but those were very small roles.

Sock Monkey is "Dwarf #8" in
"Princess Snowy & Friends"

Sock Monkey is "Chew Toy" in
"SASSIE GO HOME"

Sock Monkey is "Hapless Victim" in
"JAWZIE STRIKES YET AGAIN"

This movie was the chance of a lifetime.
Kiss or no kiss, he **had** to play Red Reardon.

Sock Monkey had to get busy and prepare. He called his friends and asked them to help.

To show Sock Monkey how to yodel, Miss Bunn took him on a crazy airplane ride. She played cowboy music while flying loop-de-loops.

Next, Froggie gave Sock Monkey a horseback riding lesson. Froggie's horse, Stardust, was thrilled to be helping such a famous actor.

And Blue Pig dressed like a cow, then ran around and around until Sock Monkey got good enough with the lasso to catch him.

Sock Buddy lent Sock Monkey one of his many sensational cowboy outfits, then helped him get all decked out.

Sock Monkey was ready to begin making his movie. Almost . . .

The next day, Sock Monkey arrived on the set of "HUBBUB AT THE HAPPY CANYON HOEDOWN."

He met the director, a very loud man.

Then he met Lulu Nevada, the actress he was supposed to kiss!

Sock Monkey tried to talk to the director about the big kiss, but . . .

the filming had begun!

Sock Monkey aced all his scenes.
He yodeled melodiously and rode his horse handsomely
and lassoed the cow skillfully. Everything was going great!

**Lunch Break!
Next Scene: The
Big Kiss!**

Sock Monkey wobbled in his boots as he walked over to his trailer. His friends had prepared a delicious lunch for him. But Sock Monkey couldn't eat.

Oooohh

Finally, it was time to film the big KISS!

Sock Monkey and Lulu began to sing . . .

and inch closer and closer together.

Lulu leaned in toward Sock Monkey . . .

Sock Monkey shuffled over to Lulu and apologized.

But no matter what he said, Lulu wept and wept.

Sock Monkey felt terrible. He realized there was only one thing he could do. . . .

Sock Monkey kissed Lulu!
Right on the cheek!

CUT!
THAT'S
PERFECT!

The filming was over! And the kiss wasn't all that bad!
Sock Monkey and Lulu would both be stars.

WE'RE ALL DONE!
IT'S A WRAP!

THE END